JAKE MAD...

D0328271

DANGER
on the REEF

BY JAKE MADDOX

Text by Natasha Deen
Illustrated by Giuliano Aloisi

STONE ARCH BOOKS
a capstone imprint

Jake Maddox Adventure is published by Stone Arch Books,
an imprint of Capstone.
1710 Roe Crest Drive
North Mankato, Minnesota 56003
www.capstonepub.com

Library of Congress Cataloging-in-Publication Data is available on
the Library of Congress website.

ISBN: 978-1-4965-8700-8 (hardcover)
ISBN: 978-1-4965-9206-4 (paperback)
ISBN: 978-1-4965-8701-5 (eBook PDF)

Summary: Jasmine Lopez and her brother, Arjun, love exploring
the coral reefs around Fiji, where their marine biologist parents
are stationed. Jasmine, already a certified scuba diver, dreams of
following in her parents' footsteps and wants to help Arjun do the
same. Unfortunately her younger brother is sure he already knows
everything. That attitude gets them into danger when Arjun drifts
too far from the group during a dive—and straight into a reef
shark.

Designer: Lori Bye

Printed in the United States of America.
PA100

TABLE OF CONTENTS

CHAPTER 1

THE COOL BLUE

Jasmine Lopez's heart was racing with excitement as she climbed from the dive boat and into the South Pacific Ocean. The warm waters closed over her head. The world above disappeared as her weight vest pulled her deeper into the water.

Jasmine adjusted the goggles on her face and looked for her mother and diving buddy, Dr. Samaira Lopez. She was easy to spot in her blue wet suit, black fins, and bright, neon-yellow mask.

Mom tapped her own arm, then gave Jasmine a thumbs-up. That was code for one of the most important rules of scuba diving: *Always stay close to your diving buddy.*

Jasmine tapped her arm in reply and returned her mom's thumbs-up. Then Mom held up six fingers.

Six fingers meant sixty feet. At twelve years old, Jasmine had been scuba diving for two years. That was the deepest she was allowed to dive. She held up six fingers in return to let Mom know she wouldn't go any deeper.

Mom gave her two thumbs-up, and Jasmine grinned. The final safety check was complete.

Now it was time for some fun in Fiji, where her parents worked as marine biologists. They were studying the best ways to help regrow the coral reefs.

Mom descended to the reef, and Jasmine followed after her. Her fins propelled her through the clear blue water. Clown fish, orange and white, darted in and out of the coral.

Jasmine swam closer to the colorful scene up ahead. Golden damselfish, defending their territory, rushed at her. They were small and not really a threat, but she loved how protective they were of their home.

I don't blame them, Jasmine thought as she swam. *The reefs need all the protection they can get.*

Nearby, Jasmine caught sight of her younger brother, Arjun. He was swimming with their dad, Dr. Antonio Lopez. Most of the time Arjun was Jasmine's diving buddy, but not today.

Thank goodness! Jasmine thought.

She loved her brother, but lately being his buddy had stopped being fun. Arjun was ten years old and had just started diving, but he already thought he knew everything. He refused to listen to Jasmine.

Even though he was supposed to stay close, Arjun would swim farther than arm's reach. He was only allowed to dive to a maximum of forty feet, but that didn't stop him from trying to go deeper. And that meant Jasmine had to chase after him.

At least he's Dad's problem today, Jasmine thought.

She exhaled through her mouth, and the bubbles from her regulator sped to the surface. Startled by the noise and movement, a golden damselfish darted from her.

Jasmine swam away and moved to check her mom's air tank. As Mom's diving buddy, that was Jasmine's responsibility.

Jasmine made sure there were more than fifty bars of pressure. That was the safety number. If the air level got down to fifty bars, the tank was only a quarter full, and it would be time to start heading for the surface.

Mom turned and pointed toward the surface. Jasmine shook her head, then spun around so Mom could check her tank too. When she felt a tap on her shoulder, Jasmine turned back.

Mom flashed her a thumbs-up. Then she pivoted toward the reef and went back to work.

Jasmine glanced over to Arjun and Dad. They were investigating a shelf of coral to the left of the reef.

Dad checked Arjun's tank and gave him the thumbs-up. Arjun did the same for their father.

Jasmine propelled herself through the water. While Mom and Dad collected data, she would do her part by removing any garbage.

Jasmine made her way around the coral. She made sure to pay close attention to the nooks and crannies.

Whitetip reef sharks loved to nap in the cozy crevices. They mostly stayed away from divers because they didn't like the noise of the bubbles from the air tanks. But that didn't mean they wouldn't get grouchy if a diver disturbed them.

Just then a nearby movement caught Jasmine's attention. She raised her head and looked to her left.

Arjun was picking up trash from the reef and putting it in his mesh bag. He stopped and watched a school of yellowfin goatfish swim past. Then he swam in between them, holding out his fingers.

Jasmine puffed out an irritated breath. Arjun knew the rule about leaving the fish alone: *Watch, don't touch.*

She was tempted to swim after Arjun. Disturbing the fish wasn't just disrespectful. It could attract sharks to their location.

But just then, Arjun swam away from the fish. He headed back to Dad.

Jasmine went back to work. She noticed a plastic six-pack ring snagged on a piece of rock and snatched it up before it could get caught on a turtle's fin.

A glint of something shiny caught her eye next. Jasmine reached for the object. It was a silver ring.

Probably an inexperienced diver, she thought.

Most divers knew not to wear anything shiny when diving. It attracted fish, which would nibble and bite, thinking the object could be food.

Jasmine stashed it in her bag so it couldn't be accidentally eaten by the marine life. When she looked up, she realized she'd moved too far from her mom.

Jasmine turned and started to swim closer. But something suddenly caught her heel and dragged her down.

CHAPTER 2

UNEXPECTED TERROR

Instinct took over. Jasmine kicked. Her heart raced, but she was ready to swim away as fast as she could or to defend herself. Maybe it was a grumpy fish. Or maybe she'd been caught in some rope or plastic.

Instead, she turned and saw Arjun.

Her brother waved at her. Then he spun and returned to their dad's side.

Furious, Jasmine followed. She tried to get her mind back on the dive, but she couldn't.

Instead of noticing the different types of fish swimming around her, Jasmine kept watching Arjun. She couldn't shake the feeling he was going to do something silly and ruin the dive.

Jasmine checked her watch. They had been underwater for thirty-five minutes and still had five minutes left on the dive. Usually she would take all the time she could get. But worrying about Arjun took the fun out of it.

Mom and Dad were still busy collecting samples of coral. Jasmine tapped her dad on his shoulder. When he turned her way, she pointed up toward the surface.

Dad nodded. Mom saw their underwater conversation and nodded too. She motioned to Arjun, and the four of them swam to the surface.

Jasmine concentrated on moving slowly. Every few feet, she exhaled.

Emptying her breath allowed her lungs to adjust to the changing pressure of the water. It also prevented nitrogen from forming in her blood, which could make her dizzy or nauseated.

Jasmine broke the surface of the water first. She pulled off her mask and took out her regulator. Blinking, she turned and saw the dive boat. Captain Brody waved at them from on board.

Mom waved back. She pulled her regulator out of her mouth and looked at Jasmine. "Is everything OK?" she asked. "Why did you stop the dive early?"

"I was hungry," Jasmine lied.

She was mad at her brother, but lately it seemed as if all she and Arjun did was fight. Jasmine was tired of it. She wanted to talk to Arjun first and give him the chance to apologize.

Besides, thought Jasmine, *I always watch Arjun when our parents are gone. If he gets grounded from diving, I'll have to babysit him. No way am I giving up the water for him!*

Dad laughed. "You're always hungry!" he said.

"Captain Brody is a great cook," Mom said. "I wouldn't mind another one of his crabmeat sandwiches." She kicked out and started for the boat.

Jasmine's dad followed. Arjun started to do the same, but Jasmine pulled him back.

"What?" Arjun snapped. He shook free and treaded the water. "What's your problem?"

"You are," said Jasmine. "What were you playing at down there?"

Arjun rolled his eyes. "I should have known you would freak out. I was just having fun, OK? It's no big deal."

"Yes, it is," Jasmine insisted. She inflated her buoyancy-control device to help stay afloat in the water while they spoke. "We're underwater. You can't go pulling me down. That's dangerous."

"No, it's not." Arjun scowled. "It was a prank. You're overreacting."

"There are sharks—"

Arjun interrupted Jasmine. "They're not going to come after us," he said. "Whitetip reef sharks sleep during the day. Besides, even if they were awake, our bubbles would scare them off."

"You don't know everything, you know," Jasmine said.

Arjun scowled. "Yeah, well neither do you," he said. "You're not the only one who wants to be a marine biologist like Mom and Dad. I know how to handle myself around the reef."

"No, you don't!" Jasmine took a sharp breath and tried to control her temper. "I saw you trying to play with the fish. You know you're not supposed to do that!"

"That didn't hurt anyone."

"It could have," Jasmine said. "If we get caught in the middle of a school of fish and a shark comes looking for food, that's a problem. The sharks won't be able to tell the difference between us and the fish. We could get seriously hurt. The bubbles from our tanks won't help."

"Kids!" Dad called to them. "What's going on?"

"Nothing!" Jasmine yelled back. "We're coming."

"No one got hurt," Arjun said. "It's fine. You need to lighten up!"

With that, he turned and swam away, heading for the boat.

Jasmine's heart sank. She and Arjun used to talk about being marine biologists together. They both dreamed of continuing their parents' work studying the reefs.

But how am I supposed to trust him with something as big as rebuilding the reefs if I can't trust him to respect the rules of scuba diving? Jasmine worried.

CHAPTER 3

JASMINE'S PLAN

"This is so exciting!" Mom exclaimed. She pulled Jasmine closer and pointed at the computer screen. "Look at all this lovely data."

Jasmine laughed. "You're the only person I know who gets excited about numbers."

Dad and Arjun walked out of the kitchen. Arjun had a plate of mango slices for everyone.

Dad came over to the computer. "Is that the latest data?" he asked, pushing his dark hair off of his forehead. "This is so exciting!"

Jasmine shook her head. "Correction," she told her mom. "You're one of only two people I know who gets excited about numbers."

"Nice try," Mom said to Jasmine. She smiled at Arjun and took a slice of fruit. "I know you love learning about how the reef is evolving and changing, Jasmine."

"I do," Jasmine admitted. "The polyps that make up the reefs are amazing."

Actually, they were beyond amazing. Polyps were tiny animals and relatives of anemones and jellyfish. They could live by themselves, or they could live in large colonies—the reefs—that became homes for other animals and plants.

"You know what's really amazing?" Dad asked as he sat down. "You and Arjun learning about the reefs together. This is a fantastic opportunity for you both."

Mom smiled in agreement. "I love that you both love the reefs as much as we do," she said. "One day all of us will dive and study the reefs together."

Jasmine laughed. "We're already doing that now."

"But just imagine how much more we'll get to do when you both have degrees in marine biology." She grabbed Arjun and covered him with kisses. "We'll write papers and give talks and do research. . . . Think of the data and numbers!"

"Too many kisses!" Arjun pulled away. "It's going to be awesome!" he continued. "I'm going to be the best marine biologist ever." He picked up a slice of mango from the plate. "I'm going outside."

How is he going to be the best marine biologist ever if he doesn't respect the wildlife? Jasmine wondered as she walked to the table.

A variety of beach finds, from seashells to sand dollars and empty snail shells, sat in rows. She traced the objects with her finger.

"What's wrong?" Dad asked, joining her at the table.

"Nothing," Jasmine said.

"Aren't you excited about us studying the reefs as a family?" Dad asked.

I want to tell Dad and Mom what's happening, Jasmine thought. *But if I do, it's going to start a fight with Arjun.*

"Of course," she said slowly. "I'm excited about becoming a marine biologist too."

"Jasmine, honey," Mom said, walking over. "I love the idea of you following in our footsteps, but if this isn't what you want—"

"No, it's not that." Jasmine took a breath. She really didn't want to get Arjun in trouble. But she needed to keep him safe so they would all be safe.

"It's Arjun," she finally said. Briefly, Jasmine told her parents what had happened underwater.

Dad looked upset. "Arjun! Come in here!" he called.

"What? I'm right here," Arjun said as he came in from the front porch.

"What is this about you playing pranks instead of helping your sister clean the reef?" Mom asked.

Arjun's eyes narrowed, and he glared in Jasmine's direction. "You told on me?" he said. "Why are you such a jerk?"

"Arjun!" Mom said. Her voice was sharp. "Apologize, right now."

"It's not like that—" Jasmine started to say to Arjun.

"Being underwater isn't a game," Mom interrupted. "You know the rules about fooling around down there."

"That doesn't mean we can't have fun," Arjun argued.

"Pulling your sister's fin isn't fun," said Dad. "It's a safety issue. What if it had fallen off? One of us would have had to dive deeper to catch it or it would become litter in the ocean."

"I wasn't going to pull it off," Arjun said.

Mom looked at him over her black-rimmed glasses. "What if she had accidentally kicked you in the face? It could have knocked off your regulator or your mask."

"I know how to put on my gear, even underwater," Arjun said with a scowl.

Dad sighed. "Son—"

Arjun spun on Jasmine. "You're a horrible sister!" he yelled. "You ruin everything!" With that, he ran out the door.

"I just want you to be safe!" Jasmine called after him. She stood to follow.

Dad put his hand on her shoulder. "It's OK, sweetheart. Let him go. I'll talk to him." He looked at Mom. "I'll get him to apologize for the name-calling too."

"I don't understand," Jasmine said after Dad had left. "Arjun and I used to be amazing diving buddies. Now all we do is fight."

"It's hard for him," Mom said. "You're older. You can dive deeper, and you get more freedom when we're diving. He just wants to prove he's as good as you."

"But I already know that!" Jasmine said.

"We know it, but Arjun doesn't." Mom sighed. "That's why we like the two of you diving together. You're a great diving buddy, and you take good care of him. The hard part is getting Arjun to understand he needs to be a great diving buddy too."

"Can't you make him understand?" Jasmine asked.

Mom shook her head. "This is something he needs to figure out for himself. But if he can't learn to behave when we're underwater, he'll have to stay on land."

Jasmine's heart sank. *Stay on land?* she thought. Arjun was too young to be left alone. *If Arjun is grounded, that means I'm grounded too. With Mom and Dad working on the reef, there's no one else left to watch him.*

She had to watch over her brother. Jasmine was going to make sure Arjun went back to being a good diving buddy—for both their sakes.

CHAPTER 4

SIBLING CONNECTION

"Come on, let's go! Let's go!" Arjun grabbed Mom and Dad by the hands. He pulled them across the warm sands to Captain Brody's boat.

Dad laughed. "We're walking as fast as we can!" he said.

Jasmine trailed after them. Her stomach churned. Arjun hadn't spoken to her all morning.

We're supposed to be swimming buddies today, she thought. *Will he listen to me?*

"Jasmine, you and Arjun check the equipment," Mom said as they all walked the gangplank onto the boat.

Once on board, Jasmine and Arjun headed to the equipment. Arjun inspected the gauge on each air tank.

"The tanks are full," he said.

"Let me double-check," said Jasmine. She cast a quick glance in her brother's direction. "Not that I don't believe you, but—"

He waved away her words. "It's good to have one person check," he said. "It's better to have two people check."

"You're not mad?" Jasmine asked.

Arjun shrugged. "Dad says it's the drill," he said. "You're just doing what you're supposed to do."

"It's to keep us safe," she tried to explain to him.

Arjun didn't say anything for a moment. Then he muttered, "I shouldn't have called you a jerk yesterday."

"Thanks," Jasmine said. He didn't sound happy, which meant he was probably still mad at her.

But at least we're not fighting, she told herself. *Maybe being his diving buddy won't be so bad after all.*

After they'd verified the air in the tanks, Jasmine and Arjun checked the regulators for leaks. Jasmine tightened the O-ring on top of one of the tanks.

Next she opened the air valve and listened. There was no hissing sound, which meant there were no air leaks.

"This one is OK," she said.

Arjun checked the remaining three tanks as Jasmine watched. After that, they made sure the vests were free of tears.

"Everything is in place," Jasmine said to their parents. "We have fins, air tanks, pressure gauges, weight belts, regulators—"

"And they're all in working condition," Arjun interrupted. "The vests don't have tears, the gauges are working, there are no leaks. And I apologized to Jasmine."

He stopped to catch his breath.

Dad laughed and held up his hands. "OK, OK, I get it," he said. "You're both working hard to show you are responsible enough to dive."

Dad rubbed Arjun's back. "Good job following up on our talk last night. I'm proud of you."

* * *

Jasmine glided underwater. Her smooth movements cut through the currents. She hovered over a section of the reef. The coral swayed back and forth.

As they dove deeper, Jasmine kept an eye on her brother. When Arjun looked her way, she tapped on her arm and gave him a thumbs-up. Arjun tapped his arm and gave her a thumbs-up.

Jasmine held up four fingers. Then she waved them, so he understood.

Forty feet, Arjun. That's as far as you're allowed to dive.

Arjun held up four fingers, then gave her two thumbs-up.

Maybe this dive will be better, Jasmine thought hopefully. *Arjun is listening to everything I say.*

She gave Arjun two thumbs-up, and together they swam to the reef. They were in a different section today, which meant more garbage to clean. Jasmine did her part to clear out the plastic bottles and bags. So did Arjun.

After a few minutes, Arjun tapped Jasmine's shoulder. He pointed to her tank and gave her a thumbs-up. Then he spun so she could check his air pressure.

Wow, Jasmine thought. *Whatever Dad said to him really worked.*

She flashed a thumbs-up and went back to checking the health of the coral. But when she looked up, she didn't see Arjun.

Panic raced through Jasmine. *Where is he?* she thought.

She spun in a circle, then spotted her brother directly behind her. Jasmine exhaled, and the air bubbled to the surface.

Just then a school of masked butterfly fish swam near Arjun. They were close enough to touch. The school of fish was also big enough to get lost in.

Jasmine resisted the urge to reach out and grab her brother.

This is his test. He knows better than to swim into the schools of fish. Keep your distance, Arjun.

From the corner of her eye, Jasmine watched her parents. If they turned around and saw Arjun moving into the school of fish, it was all over. He'd be grounded on land—and Jasmine with him.

Arjun moved. Instead of giving into the temptation to play with the fish, he swam to his sister. Jasmine held up her hand for an underwater high five.

Way to go, Arjun! she thought. *Maybe he's going to make a good diving buddy again after all.*

CHAPTER 5

SHARK!

Three days later, Jasmine wondered if she'd been wrong to believe her brother could behave on a dive. She'd spent most of yesterday chasing after him. He'd swum away from her several times during their dive and kept trying to play with the fish.

"What is going on with you?" Jasmine asked Arjun. They were on the dive boat and slipping on their fins. "You were doing great. Now you're back to your bad habits."

"I'm not a baby, Jasmine," Arjun said. "Stop treating me like one. I'm doing what you asked about the scuba checks and picking up the garbage. So what if I want to have a little fun by diving a little deeper?"

"It's not safe for you to dive as deep as I do," Jasmine said.

Arjun rolled his eyes. "It's just a couple of feet. Geez. I'm just as good at diving as you are. You just don't want to admit it." He walked away from her.

Jasmine spied her dad coming on deck. "Can I be your dive buddy today?" she asked.

"I thought you and Arjun were diving together today," said Dad. He frowned. "Is something going on?"

If I tell Dad what Arjun is doing, Arjun will have to stay on the boat, Jasmine thought. *Then I'll have to stay on the boat too.*

She forced a smile. "Nope, it's all good. I just like swimming with you."

Dad smiled back at her. "Tomorrow, OK?" he said.

Sure, Jasmine thought glumly. *Tomorrow.*

* * *

The sunlight lit up the colors of the reef. But it didn't spotlight the person Jasmine was looking for—Arjun.

Jasmine checked over her shoulder for her brother. *Where is he?* She didn't see him anywhere. Then she looked down.

There was Arjun, diving deeper than he was allowed. Jasmine glanced at her parents. They were focused on taking readings of the coral.

They're trusting me to watch over Arjun, Jasmine thought. *If they see what's happening, we'll both be in trouble.*

Arjun looked up and saw her. Jasmine waved at him to join her. But instead of listening, Arjun swam up and left—straight toward a school of yellowfin goatfish.

Jasmine swam quickly toward her brother. She had to stop him. The current pushed her hard against the reef, scraping her arm. It hurt, but she couldn't worry about that now.

Arjun swam into the middle of the fish. He reached out and tried to touch them.

That's it! Jasmine thought, swimming hard and fast toward her brother. *I'm taking him to the surface. And I'm telling Mom and Dad I don't want to be his buddy anymore. He never listens!*

Jasmine broke into the middle of the activity. There were so many fish, it was difficult to find Arjun. The fish's silver scales glinted in the water and kept the reef hidden from view.

Jasmine swam among them, looking for her brother. When she spotted him, she grabbed Arjun by the shoulder and pointed toward the reef. Arjun shook his head and gave her a thumbs-down.

The fish swirled and moved around them. Bubbles from Jasmine's and Arjun's regulators sped upward. Some of the fish darted away.

Jasmine pointed to the reef again, then pointed to the surface. Arjun turned away.

For a heart-stopping second, Jasmine thought he'd swim from her. *What will I do then?* she worried. *It's not like I can call Mom and Dad for help.*

Jasmine forced herself to take a breath and exhaled. She reached for her brother, but he was already turning back to her.

Arjun pointed to the reef, and Jasmine blew out another breath. *He's listening—finally.*

Brother and sister swam carefully toward the edge of the school of fish. The reef was just ahead. But Jasmine stopped short when she realized what was blocking their path—a whitetip reef shark.

The shark had been drawn in by the activity. Now it was looking for food, and Jasmine and Arjun stood in its way.

CHAPTER 6

STOP, THINK, BREATHE, ACT

Once the shark started feeding, it wouldn't know the difference between Jasmine, Arjun, and the fish. It would just be focused on eating.

Don't panic, Jasmine thought. *You know the drill. Stop, think, breathe, act.* Stop where you are, think about what needs to be done, take a breath, then act.

Think, Jasmine told herself. The best thing was to get out of the column. Swim down and around. Most of all, stay with Arjun.

Jasmine inhaled and let out a long breath. That helped calm her racing heart. Then she reached for Arjun. If she could hold on to his vest, she could make sure they didn't get separated.

But Arjun, already scared, panicked when Jasmine touched him. He jerked sideways, shoving her aside. As he kicked away, his fin caught Jasmine's mask and ripped it off.

Jasmine snatched the mask before it could sink away. She put the mask back on, but it was full of water.

Quickly, she tilted into a forty-five degree angle, pressing her thumb against her forehead to hold the mask in place. Then she took a breath through her regulator.

Instead of breathing out of her mouth, Jasmine exhaled through her nose. Since her nose was covered by the mask, the bubbles filled the space. As they bubbled into the mask, they pushed the water out from the bottom.

There! Now I can see again! Jasmine thought, looking around. She spotted Arjun trying to swim away from the shark.

Jasmine sped to her brother and grabbed his vest, pulling him down. Then she swam away from the fish in a horizontal path.

Once they were out of the range of the school, Jasmine looked toward the surface. She kept an eye on the shark.

So far, so good, she thought. *It's concentrating on the yellowfin goatfish.*

Holding tight to Arjun, Jasmine swam toward the surface. She made sure she exhaled to equalize the pressure in her lungs. Every few feet, she poked Arjun in the side. The sharp movement forced him to exhale, ensuring he didn't get any nitrogen in his blood.

The water grew brighter as they climbed higher. Finally, they broke the surface.

Jasmine yanked the cord of Arjun's buoyancy-control device. His vest inflated. She did the same thing to her vest. Once they were safely floating, she let him have it.

Jasmine pulled the regulator out of her mouth. "What were you thinking?" she exclaimed. "Do you have any idea how dangerous that was? We could have been seriously hurt!"

"I'm sorry!" Arjun was crying. "I just wanted to see the fish."

"You did see them! The problem was you wanted to play with them. They're not pets, Arjun." Jasmine knew she was yelling, but she couldn't help it. The encounter had been terrifying. "They're wild creatures, and you have to respect them. And you have to respect their space!"

"I know!" Arjun said. He hiccupped. "I'm sorry!"

"Stop crying." Jasmine snapped to cover her fear. "I have to think about what to do next."

"Maybe we should swim back to the boat," Arjun said, sounding scared.

Mom and Dad are still underwater," Jasmine said. "I have no idea if they saw what happened. I don't know if we should swim back to where they are or go to the boat."

As she thought, Jasmine treaded water. She looked toward the dive boat, hoping to see Captain Brody.

Sure enough, Jasmine spotted him. Captain Brody stood on deck, waving his arms in the air. Jasmine squinted. No, he wasn't waving. He was pointing.

"Jasmine! Jasmine!" Arjun pulled her arm. He was pointing too.

Jasmine looked over her shoulder. There were three shark fins poking out of the water. And they were coming in their direction.

CHAPTER 7

ALONE IN THE WATER

"Sharks." Jasmine gulped. "Why are there sharks up here?"

"Jasmine, your arm," said Arjun. He pointed again, this time at her.

Jasmine looked down. There, in the clear waters, was a thin trickle of red.

"Oh, no!" she realized. "I bumped up against the reef when I was swimming after you. I must have ripped my suit and cut my arm."

Jasmine gently pulled at the neoprene material to check her cut. It didn't look too deep, but sharks had a keen sense of smell. They could smell blood from a quarter of a mile away.

"I'm so sorry," Arjun said. "This is all my fault."

"It's my fault too," Jasmine said. "I was so mad at you that I wasn't paying attention. I hit the reef, and I cut myself."

Arjun pointed to the fins in the water. "What do we do?" he asked.

"I don't know." Jasmine swallowed the lump in her throat. Arjun wasn't the only one who wanted to cry.

"Yes, you do," Arjun told her. "You always know. You're a great diver and a great diving buddy."

Jasmine shook her head. Tears blurred her vision as she stared at the sharks.

"I thought I did the right thing getting us up here," she said. "But I was wrong. Look at the sharks! I should have swum back to the reef. I should have taken us to Mom and Dad, but the shark was blocking our path."

"Think, Jasmine," said Arjun.

Jasmine was having a hard time breathing. She wasn't sure what to do. She pulled anxiously at her vest.

"Jasmine! The sharks!" Arjun said. "Think!"

Arjun's words and his fear snapped Jasmine out of her frozen state. She was his diving buddy. He was counting on her.

Stop, think, breathe, act, Jasmine reminded herself. She took in a long breath, held it, then let it out. She blinked away the tears. The sharks came into focus.

Jasmine watched the sharks swimming. They didn't seem to be moving any closer.

"They're not interested in us," she realized. "They're interested in the school of fish we left."

"Should we dive back to Mom and Dad?" Arjun asked.

Jasmine spun him around and looked at the bars on his tank. "No," she said. "You have less than fifty bars. You don't have enough air to dive."

She looked up and saw the boat heading to them. "Come on," she said to Arjun. "Let's swim away from this spot and give the sharks distance. Captain Brody will come and get us."

Suddenly there was a bubbling sound behind them. Jasmine and Arjun spun around. A moment later, Mom and Dad broke the surface of the water.

"Mom! Dad!" Arjun swam to their parents.

"Are you OK?" Dad asked as he inflated his buoyancy-control device.

"I think so," said Jasmine. "The sharks seem busy with the fish."

Mom's lips were pressed into a tight, angry line. "I saw you trying to play with the fish, Arjun. I'm glad everyone is safe, but this should never have happened. Swim to the boat. We need to have a family discussion."

CHAPTER 8

DIVING BUDDIES

Back on the boat, the family sat in a circle on the sunny deck. Jasmine was still shaken from their near-miss in the water.

"I looked up from the reef and saw you swimming into the school of fish," Mom said to Arjun. "You know that's against the rules."

Arjun opened his mouth to speak, but Mom held up her hand. Arjun nodded and pulled his legs to his chest.

"I tapped your dad on the shoulder, and raced toward you." She looked over at Jasmine. "Jasmine was already on her way."

"I couldn't believe what I saw," Dad said. "We've talked to you kids about respecting the underwater life. This is their territory." He shook his head. "Swimming right into the middle of the school of fish. Arjun, I'm so disappointed."

Arjun blinked fast and swallowed. "I'm sorry," he whispered.

"This is why we observe marine life, but we leave the animals alone," said Mom.

"We tried to get to you," Dad said. "But there were so many fish, and you got lost. We didn't know where you were until we saw you swimming to the surface. Do you know how terrified we were for you?"

"I'm so relieved nothing terrible happened," Mom said.

But it could have," Dad said to Arjun. Sharks, fish, and the other marine life have to be respected. There will be consequences for your behavior."

"Arjun, you'll stay on the ship with the boat crew," said Mom. "You can help me or your dad organize the data we collect. You can also brush up on your reading about the reef and remind yourself how much it needs to be respected."

"For how long?" Arjun asked.

"Until you can be trusted to respect the ocean and its inhabitants," said Dad. "How long that is will be up to you."

"You'll have to show us you can be responsible," said Mom.

"What about me?" Jasmine asked. "Does that mean I have to stay on the ship too?"

"No, of course not," said Mom. "Why would you think that?"

"I usually babysit him if you guys go out," Jasmine said.

Dad shook his head. "This is different," he said. "Arjun needs to deal with the consequences of his behavior. You didn't do anything wrong, Jasmine. We wouldn't ground you from the dive."

Hearing her dad's words, Jasmine realized he was right. This situation was different.

Jasmine sighed. *If only I'd talked to Mom and Dad sooner,* she thought. *We could have solved the Arjun problem days ago!*

"While Arjun is on the boat, you'll dive with your mom or me," Dad added. "I'm proud of what you did to help your brother and to get yourselves out of a scary situation."

"Arjun helped me too," she said. "When I panicked, he calmed me down." She put her hand on her brother's shoulder. "You were a great diving buddy."

Arjun shook his head. "No, I wasn't," he said. "If I'd been a great diving buddy, I wouldn't have bothered the fish or gone deeper in the water. I'm sorry, Jasmine. I could have really gotten us hurt. I promise, from now on, I'll be the best diving buddy you've ever had. Once I'm allowed back in the water, that is."

Jasmine grinned. "Thanks, Arjun. I'm going to be your best diving buddy too. And I'm going to start right now. How about if we get those books on the reef and start reading?"

"Really?" Arjun asked. "You don't mind spending the afternoon with me instead of diving?"

"I don't mind at all," Jasmine said. "We're buddies, in and out of the water."

AUTHOR BIO

Natasha Deen loves stories—exciting ones, scary ones, and especially funny ones! She lives in Edmonton, Alberta, Canada, with her family, where she writes stories for kids of all ages. When she's not writing or visiting schools and libraries, Natasha spends a lot of her time trying to convince her pets that she's the boss of the house.

ILLUSTRATOR BIO

After graduating from the Institute for Cinema and Television in Rome, Italy, in 1995, Giuliano Aloisi began working as an animator, layout artist, and storyboard artist, on several TV series and TV games for RAI TV. He went on to illustrate for the comic magazine *Lupo Alberto* and for *Cuore*, a satirical weekly magazine. Giuliano continues to work as an animator and illustrator for advertising companies and educational publishing.

GLOSSARY

buoyancy (BOI-yuhn-see)—the tendency of an object to float or rise when submerged in a liquid

cranny (KRAN-ee)—a small opening or space

crevice (KREV-is)—a narrow opening or crack in a hard surface and especially in rock

gauge (GAYJ)—a dial or instrument used to measure something, such as an engine's temperature

horizontal (hor-uh-ZON-tuhl)—side to side

inhabitant (in-HAB-i-tuhnt)—a person or animal that lives in a place

instinct (IN-stingkt)—behavior that is natural rather than learned

keen (KEEN)—the ability to notice things easily

litter (LIT-ur)—pieces of paper or other garbage that are scattered around carelessly

neoprene (NEE-uh-preen)—a strong, waterproof material used to make wet suits

nitrogen (NYE-truh-juhn)—a colorless, odorless gas

opportunity (op-er-TOO-ni-tee)—a chance for greater success

polyp (POL-ip)—a small sea animal with a tubular body and a round mouth surrounded by tentacles

pressure (PRESH-ur)—the force produced by pressing on something

reef (REEF)—a strip of rock, coral, or sand near the surface of the ocean

regulator (REG-yoo-lay-tuhr)—a piece of equipment that allows divers to breathe air from an air tank

DISCUSSION QUESTIONS

1. Based on this story and any other experiences you've had, do you think scuba diving is exciting or scary? Explain your reasoning, and talk about if it's an activity you'd like to try.

2. Do you think Jasmine made the right choice by not talking to her parents about Arjun's pranks and misbehavior? Why or why not? Why do you think she was so determined to protect her little brother?

3. Jasmine and Arjun are both scared when they run into a shark in the water. How would you have reacted if you'd been there? Talk about some other ways they could have dealt with their shark encounter.

WRITING PROMPTS

1. Imagine you are exploring the coral reefs of Fiji with Jasmine and her family. Write a few paragraphs about your experience. What do you see? What do you hear? How do you feel?

2. When they are diving with their parents, Jasmine and Arjun help the oceans by clearing litter from the reefs. What are some other ways we can help coral reefs stay healthy and thrive? Write a list of some of those actions. (Your library will have nonfiction books to help you.)

3. Jasmine and Arjun both dream of being marine biologists when they grow up. Write a paragraph about what you want to be when you grow up, whether that's a marine biologist or something else.

MORE ABOUT
SCUBA DIVING

Humans have long been curious about life below the surface of the ocean. But explorations were limited due to a lack of equipment allowing humans to breathe underwater. That changed in the 1940s thanks to two people: explorer Jacques Cousteau and engineer Émile Gagnan.

Cousteau and Gagnan created a device called the Aqua-Lung. The Aqua-Lung let people dive for longer periods of time and go deeper than ever before. This device allowed scuba diving to become a popular activity. These days, humans can explore underwater caves, meet creatures that live deep in the ocean, and investigate coral reefs.

If you ever go diving, you'll need the right gear. Below is a list of equipment you might use when exploring these underwater marvels:

air tank—something that is strapped to a diver's vest, then to his or her back, and carries filtered air (not pure oxygen) through the regulator to the diver

buoyancy-control device—usually in a jacket style, this contains an inflatable bladder to help divers float while on the surface or to help them stay weightless under the water

fins—made of rubber, these attach to a diver's feet to help propel him or her through the water

mask—something a diver wears over his or her face to protect and keep water out of the eyes and nose

O-ring—a device used in regulators, tanks, and lights that helps prevent leaks and breaks due to the pressure

pressure gauge—a device that monitors the pressure in an air tank and ensures a diver has enough air for a dive

regulator—a piece that delivers filtered air from the air tank to a diver's mouth

snorkel—a small tube used by a diver to breathe while underwater

weight belt—used with a buoyancy-control device, this heavy belt wraps around a diver's waist and helps him or her sink lower into the water